a lovely menace

A DARK, AGE GAP AND FORBIDDEN ROMANCE

SHANJIDA NUSRATH ALI

Copyright © Shanjida Nusrath Ali, 2023

All Rights Reserved.

ISBN: 9798854541619

This book or any portion thereof may not be reproduced or used in any matter whatsoever without the express written permission of the authors except for the use of brief quotations in a book review. This is a work of fiction. All names, characters, business, events and places are either the product of the authors' imagination or used fictitiously.

Editor: Helena Dautrive, BookBish Edits
Instagram handle: @book.b.ish
Website: https://beacons.ai/book.b.ish

playlist

Breathe- Fleurie, Tommee Profitt
Black Sea- Natasha Blume
Let Go- Ark Patrol, Veronika Redd
I Wanna Be Yours- NVBR, Xanemusic
Pain & Pleasure- Black Atlass
Like U- Rosenfled
I Want To- Rosenfled
After Dark- Mr. Kitty
Do It For Me- Rosenfled

warning

The book contains explicit sex scenes, foul language, rape, physical abuse, drug abuse, mention of cannibalism, murder, violence, and religious references. Reader discretion is advised.

PROLOGUE

1972, Vailburg

My heart raced faster and faster with every passing second. Every breath I inhaled burned my lungs. Every step I took made me wish to turn back time, so I would never be born in the first place, especially in a horrific and fucked up place like this.

But I had no choice. I was bound to this darkness like an innocent victim tied in a dark cellar with no way out.

When the wooden portcullis door came into my view, I felt nearly out of breath. I halted close to the door and listened to the deep faint group of chanting from inside.

With my trembling hand raised, I held the rustic iron knocker and tapped it against the wooden surface three times. Instantly a small window snapped opened with gray eyes greeting me, followed by a suspicious look.

Letting out a shaky breath, I tried to calm down my nerves even though it felt pointless.

"We are God's children, and He protects us from Evil," I muttered.

His eyes narrowed for a second before he gave a firm nod and opened the door, guiding me to the pathway of my living hell.

The chanting was replaced with pin-drop silence. Every

pair of eyes landed upon me, analyzing me from top to bottom with an emotionless gaze. They were all part of this darkness, and none carried an ounce of sanity to comprehend how wrong all of this was. I walked ahead, keeping my eyes cast down with fear starting to crawl back to my beating heart. I didn't have to look around my surroundings because I had seen it a million times.

Nothing had ever changed. The brick walls had algae and black discoloration on some parts, but there used to be a script painted on the walls that still ran in my mind. The benches lined up into two rows with a black carpet in the center that led to the end of the room. There were no windows or other doors. The candelabras were the only source of light here, hanging on either side of the walls.

Breathe. Breathe. Breathe.

I kept reminding myself as I got closer to the small stage before I stopped in front of the man responsible for all of this.

"Welcome, my child," he muttered in a deep gruff voice, sending chills down my spine. Just his voice was enough to make goosebumps form on my skin from anxiety and fear. He was dressed in all black: black shirt, black pants, and black shoes, with his folded sleeves showing off his pale, lightly bruised skin. He always wore singular-colored attire. His

cross-chain necklace hung around his neck like it usually did. But today, I couldn't see his face as it hid behind a vast animal skull, symbolizing true evil and darkness he wore like a crown. His eyes were difficult to see through the hollowed eye sockets of the head. The giant curved horns made him look like the Devil.

"Let's not waste more time," he announced and took a step back. "Turn around and serve them, my child."

I turned to face everyone in the room. I swallowed the lump in my throat and reached behind for the zipper of my white dress. With one soft push, my dress cascaded down on the floor as I tilted my face to meet everyone's cold neutral eyes while I stood naked and...vulnerable.

I felt rough ice-cold hands on my shoulders, and without seeing, I knew to whom they belonged.

"It's time for you all to serve the Angel," his order echoed through the room.

They all nodded in unison and started to get ready with calculative movements. All the women came towards me, forming a circle with their hands joined together and closed their eyes, tilting their heads back.

"Accept our service, Angel. Accept our service, Angel," they chanted with a low voice as if praying from the depths of their heartless souls.

a lovely menace

The men came forward without any clothes and had their heads covered in animal skulls.

"Accept our touch, Angel. Help us. Accept us," they muttered.

One of the men came forward with a bowl of blood before he coated his hands with it a bit and passed it to another man. With his blood-smeared hands, he stood in front of me and glided the blood from my shoulders to my breasts before giving them a light squeeze and descending to my belly and legs.

Disgust and shame were shadowing me, as my heart thrummed faster and faster. The sight of my body made me feel horrified that I wanted to throw up. My eyes were starting to water, but I knew none of them would feel an ounce of pity for me.

Another man stepped forward, pushing me by my shoulder and urging me to kneel. When I did, they surrounded me and started to take off their clothes until they all stood naked with their cocks turning hard. Some began to grab my breasts, some caressed my hair, some sat beside me and drew their hands towards the apex of my thighs...and some started stroking themselves just from my sight.

"Do you accept their service, Angel?" the familiar voice of my brother asked with a dominant tone.

No. I don't and I never will.

I wanted to say those words so badly, but I was well aware that if I declined them, there would be consequences.

I simply nodded, letting out a shaky breath, and a lone tear streamed down my cheek. "I accept."

Before I knew it, my head was held by one of the men, and my mouth was penetrated by his cock. I instantly gagged and suppressed the urge to vomit. I felt multiple hands roaming my body without my consent, and two pairs of hands caressing my cunt and even pushing a finger in. I felt my hands being used to stroke the men standing.

But a chilling fright overcame my body, and I could sense what was coming next because soon I felt the sharpness of a knife against my neck. On instinct, my body tried to be free from being killed, but the people around me kept me in place as the knife slit my throat; indescribable pain made me its prey. I screamed with my eyes wide open, but my agony was unheard as the men assaulted me while someone was cutting my head from my body.

My blood spurt out, making my entire body feel weak and fragile. My vision started to turn blurry, my heart pacing at full speed was suddenly slowing down, so I could count the beats at one point.

"You are an Angel. A true Angel…"

Those were the last words I heard before I lost all sensation, along with my soul, as forever darkness engulfed me in its arms.

I knew this was what fate had written for me. I was dying like a nobody. I was also aware of what would happen to my dead body from my murderers.

They would continue cutting my dead body, using my parts for their pleasure, and even coming on me. They still wouldn't have remorse.

But I had no choice in this. I had to do this.

shanjida nusrath ali

CHAPTER 1

SILAS

1984, Vailburg

I woke up with a jolt. My breathing is accelerating, and my heart races against my chest. Sweat coats my forehead as my gaze stops at the rotten and moldy ceiling of the prison cell, I have been in for a few months now. A bright light flashes by my cell from the central watchtower, where we are watched twenty-four hours inside this spherical building. Swallowing the lump in my throat, I sit up and get off the bed, pacing back and forth to relax my mind.

I'm sick and tired of these nightmares haunting me every night, ripping me away from a peaceful sleep.

Suddenly, I hear a loud thudding sound coming from the corner cell, followed by a man screaming.

"Ah! Ah! Ah! Let me out! I want to be out! Ah!" he yells like a maniac at the top of his lungs.

The light shines straight into his cell. The rest of the prisoners wake up and watch him slamming his head against the bars with blood dripping down his face. But he doesn't stop. His eyes are wild, his skin pale, and his bones show from being malnourished. The entrance door on the ground floor opens and *she* rushes in dressed in a white chemise.

Aella.

The prison nun who lives here to pray to God for our sins. Each prisoner visits her room and sits in the confessional as we reveal our sins and crimes to her while she sits behind a sheer black curtain. But tonight, she comes for a different purpose.

She heads to the man, still screaming, and I feel my heart racing from a sudden worry for her. *What if she gets hurt?*

I hold onto my cell's bars as I watch Aella enter the man's cell and grabs onto his arms, dragging him deeper into his cell. A part of me feels jealous of the man getting to feel her touch.

"I said let me go! I want to leave!"

"It's going to be okay, Jason. Shh," Aella tries to calm him down in her shrill, soft voice.

"No! No! No! Ah!" His cries continue, but a few seconds later, they abruptly stop.

I swallow, feeling a tad suffocated with the silence, but it breaks when Aella steps out of the cell before locking it and making her way in my direction. With each step she takes, I feel my nerves racing. Her ocean eyes meet mine as she walks by my cell. Her floral fragrance wafts around my nostrils, making my body warm and alive. I sense she feels the same because she looks over her shoulder with her almond skin suddenly flushed. Noticing my gaze, she instantly looks away and rushes downstairs to her room.

The day I came here, I was instantly astonished by her beauty. I was speechless for several seconds during my first confession because her beautiful face spellbound me to her.

And deep down, I have this urge to be with her…to make her mine. I don't care if I am fifteen years older than her or the fact she is a nun who keeps her distance from men. All I know is that my mind and soul yearn for her.

My racing heart thuds harder against my chest as I gulp, feeling breathless. Opting to lie down, I shut my eyes to get some sleep. However, this time the nightmares escape and are replaced by visions of Aella, where I imagine her naked and writhing under my touch.

***

All of the prisoners stand in a line outside the bathroom as usual. Some scratched their heads, and some smelled like rotten rats for not being given the privilege to shower for weeks. When prisoners protest or cause a disturbance, they are punished severely by being kept in isolation in the underground cellar. Most of the time, the prisoners are quiet and still, like lifeless beings. Some act like lunatics all of a sudden, loosing sense of their actions. But few hours later they act normal as if nothing happened.

I have heard of Blackwell Prison several times amongst my acquaintances but never gave much thought to it. Who knew I would end up here with life sentence?

The prison is in the remote areas of Vailburg that few people visit. Myths about mysterious murders and people going missing from here have been heard. Vast and distant mountains surround us, with the weather being cold and gloomy most of the time. It's as if the place was never offered an ounce of natural sunlight. Most of the mountains or fields are barren with dead grass and crops.

However, the building is the only enormous architecture here. It is a circular, glass-roofed structure with three floors and a watch tower within the building. Every floor has five to six prisoners, with guards stationed on every floor. But at night, the watchtower is the only security that keeps constant surveillance over us.

Prisoners are treated like scum of the earth here. The guards constantly beat prisoners for minor infractions and food is scarce. The guards also mentally abuse prisoners, taunting them of the crimes they committed and how their souls will rot in hell. A constant reminder of their meaningless lives here. Everything about this place is questionable and disturbing but I don't let it bother me. After all, I have to spend the rest of my life here for the sins I've committed.

"Did you hear that guy from last night was dragged out of his cell this morning," I hear one of the prisoners whispering behind me.

"I heard him screaming before that nun came in, but I don't know what happened," another responds.

"Me either, and this can only mean one thing."

He is dead. From the rumors I have heard, no one leaves this place alive. You either get killed by the guards or spend the rest of your life here.

"But I wish the nun came into my cell. If she did, I could have a go on that beautiful ass," he joked and lightly chuckled. My blood boils from his crude comment, especially when his friend joins in.

"I would have tagged teamed with you. It's been months since I've had a good fuck. I bet she is a virgin. I could only imagine how tight her pussy would feel."

I clench my fists together, closing my eyes as I try to zone them out before I do something disastrous.

"How about we bribe the guards at night and get into her room? It's worth a try if I get to fuck all her holes-"

The fucker doesn't get to finish his sentence as I turn around with a thunderous look, and without thinking, I punch him across his face.

With a grunt, he falls instantly on the floor and tries to get up. "What the fuck!"

His friend pushes me against my chest. "What the fuck is your problem, asshole?"

Holding the guy's head, I slam it against the wall, and he immediately falls unconscious. I straddle the other guy and grab him by his collar. I land hit after hit until his blood covers my knuckles. A crowd forms around me as they cheer for me like this is entertainment for them.

But my rage triggers me to punch harder as the thought of this fucker daring to touch Aella makes me want to kill him.

"Silas! Stop it! Stop!" Her soothing voice pulls me out of this dark void as I look up and meet her terrified eyes.

The guards come in as well as they try to clear out the crowd, and soon, I'm getting beaten constantly with their wooden batons.

"No, stop it! Don't hurt him!" Aella pleads with them, but it doesn't stop them. I grunt from pain and fall onto my back, feeling the excruciating hits on my back, sides, and head. I can feel the blood running down my face and bruises forming.

"That is enough! Stop this!" She continues begging

them to stop hurting me.. Her voice's sadness and worry are evident and it makes my heart ache.

A blow to the head from one of the guard's baton hurts my head badly as weakness takes over my body. And soon, my mind accepts the darkness.

CHAPTER 2

AELLA

Twisting the wet cloth into the small pot, I bring it to Silas's temple, wiping away the excess blood from the beating. He remains still as I clean his wounds and apply myrrh extract to help him heal.

When I'm done, I lean back and avoid looking at him. But something within me urges me to admire his forbidden beauty.

The brass oil lamp is the only light that provides me with the sight of his naked, muscular chest. His abs constrict with his heavy breathing, making my throat dry. My gaze skates up to his neck, then to his sharp jawline, covered with a five o'clock shadow. His lips are light pink, but I can't control myself from imagining about kissing them. And I wish I could see his ocean eyes that always sets an unknown calmness within me… they are a beacon of hope for me in this cave of darkness.

He is shrouded with scars and bruises, making his body look more rugged. He looks damaged and yet he is a sight to behold.

No, Aella. This is wrong. God won't forgive you for it.

My sanity keeps reprimanding me as I look away. Silas is here for murdering his wife and another man. I even heard how he tortured his wife and cut her to pieces before he killed her, which made me wary of him. I remember the first time I heard him in the confessional as I sat behind the net wall. I could hear the loneliness in his voice. I could sense how broken he felt, yet there is a sadistic side to him that even he isn't aware of.

I heard the light screeching sound of the wooden chair as the next prisoner sat down. I took the file that sat beside me and went through it quickly. His name is Silas Frost, a 35 years old ex-oil tycoon. He is fifteen years older than me. The accusations state that he killed his close friend and business partner, Liam. His company faced losses and eventually shut down. At another prison, serving his sentence for murdering Liam, he escaped one night and killed his wife. No one knows why, but the conspiracies were endless. Because of his wife's murder and Liam's, he's been sentenced to life imprisonment at Blackwell Prison.

I put away the file, sit back, and wait for him to speak.

He cleared his throat. "Um, I'm not a religious person, but I just want to get this over with. Uh...Forgive me, father, for I have sinned-"

"It's not father. I'm a nun," *I corrected him. His voice was gruff and deep, but something about it sent shivers down my spine.*

He was silent for a few minutes before I noticed his head facing my direction as he tried to get a peek at my face through the holes of the divider. "You aren't supposed to see me. Tell me the sins you have committed. Let me help you absolve yourself from the guilt."

I heard him chuckle which made me frown. This was my first time hearing a criminal chuckle at his own sins. "Why are you laughing?"

"You can't help absolve me from the guilt that I don't carry. I have no remorse for what I did," *he admitted.* "I wouldn't even call it a sin when I was trapped in it in the first place by the people I least expected from."

"Are you saying you don't feel guilty?" *I ask him.*

"I did murder my wife, but my close friend...I guess I will never know." *There was a hint of sadness in his tone, and my heart ached for him.* "I never expected my life to turn out like this, but I'm only guilty about not making the right choices at the right time."

The misery in his voice was clear as if he had lost hope for a better life. The thought made me feel sorry for him.

"Can I ask you something?" *he questioned me.*

"Yes."

"Can I see you?"

My brows furrowed in confusion from his odd request.

"Why?"

"I don't know, but I have this urge to see the person who is brave enough to hear about my suppressed thoughts and the sins I committed. Not everyone is strong enough to hear others' misery and crimes."

I swallowed, feeling my breathing turn shallow. I shouldn't be doing this, yet I can't help but get up and leave my side. "You may leave now."

I heard him get up and push away the door of his side as we come face to face. I felt all the air leaving my lungs as I stared at him. But the way his heated gaze looked at me, top to bottom, made my cheeks flush. No one had ever looked at me in such a way. It was as if he was undressing me with his eyes. I could feel a sudden electricity between us that I wanted to explore.

I could also see that he felt the same, but we both kept our secrets silent. Before he could say something, a knock on the door made me take a few steps back.

"It's time for you to go," I told him as I squirmed under his intense gaze.

He stood close to me, and I could feel his warm breath fanning my cheek as he whispered. "And here I thought I would make this as a one-time thing. But now, I will be coming again and again," he promised before walking past me with our hands touching each other for a fleeting moment. I gasped from his sudden touch as butterflies fluttered in my stomach.

Oh, God. He was the definition of sin and trouble.

He kept his promise. He visited every day while I started to feel something for him…something forbidden… something I should stop.

His soft grunts shift my gaze towards him, finding Silas waking up gradually.

His eyelids flutter open, he looks over at me, and a soft look passes his face when he sees me. My presence comforts him. I am in my habit, but a smirk pulls his lips, appreciating my appearance despite being covered.

"How are you feeling?" I whisper while avoiding his intense stare. Every time this man looks at me, my entire body tingles with forbidden sensations.

"Much better," he rasps.

"The myrrh is working its magic I suppose," I responded.

"It's the magic of your presence, Aella. Every pain or darkness I feel vanishes whenever you are around me."

I gulp, wriggling my hands together from nervousness. "You shouldn't say such things."

He sits up on his elbows. "Why? You tell us to reveal our hidden thoughts to you, and this is me doing that. Revealing the deepest secrets, I have towards you."

I shake my head and start to get up. But he catches my wrist, making me halt and gasp. His warm touch makes my lungs burn for air. He grunts as he sits up and gazes at me—his shadow dances behind him from the flickering light of the lamp. My shadow hides my face and the emotion I am going through. But his heated eyes tell me he knows what I'm feeling.

"Don't look at me like that," I begged in a hushed voice, feeling his grip tighten around my wrist.

"An alluring woman like you should be admired day and night, Aella. And I don't have any shame or regret appreciating your beauty. I can look at you for hours and not get tired," he mutters in his gruff voice, which makes my heart thump against my chest.

"I know being with you is like inviting danger but it's hard to stay away from a lovely menace like you."

Dear God.

I pull away from him, heading to the small table against the dark stone wall as I fetch a glass of water for him. Calming my racing nerves with a task, I pass him the glass and keep a distance.

As he drinks, he smirks at me. "If you think a few inches of distance will keep me away, then you are dead wrong, my love."

My love. No one has ever called me that.

"The bars keep you away," I mutter with a teasing tone.

"There are no bars now." He stands up, walking towards me as I step back against the wall. He places his hands on either side of my face and cages me. My breathing increases from his closeness while the sight of his muscular chest and arms makes me gulp.

"You should…" I struggle with my words. His eyes drop onto my cross-chain necklace before he hooks a finger on it and pulls my face closer to him.

"I should what, my love?" His hot breath feathers against my cheek, making my eyes close. Dear God, save me from this sin.

"You shouldn't have gotten yourself in that fight. Look where that got you."

He lightly chuckles under his breath. "If getting beat allows me to have you all alone to myself, then I should do it more often."

I frown. "Don't say that. And you shouldn't have fought with your inmates; they didn't deserve-"

"Trust me, Aella; they definitely deserved it. They dared to disrespect you and thought they had the right to touch you. If they do it, they will die next time."

"Disrespect me?" I asked him.

"They are monsters that will taint an innocent soul like you. But I will always be here to protect you," he promises.

"Angels are supposed to be the guardians. They will protect me."

His gaze darkens, followed by a dark smirk. "I am no angel, Aella, but this devil will protect you like no other. For you, I will sacrifice my heart, soul, and everything. Ask me for anything, my love, and I will bestow it at your feet."

I turn speechless at his confession and the raw emotions his words hold. "But…why me?"

Before he can answer my question, there is a knock at the door, making me gasp and try to escape Silas's touch. I open the door to find Julian, the head guard, and his other men waiting with grim looks.

"Are his wounds taken care of?" he asks in a cold tone.

I nod.

"Take him away," he orders the other guards to get Silas.

They barge in and grab Silas by his arms and cuff his hands, but his gaze remains on me. He doesn't protest as he is dragged out. As he leaves, he keeps looking at me over his shoulder with his intense gaze. Even when he is out of sight, I can feel his presence still in my room. His scent lingers in the air as I sit on the bed, taking off my veil. My entire body feels warm. I touch my cross-chain necklace where his touch was and close my eyes, imagining him in front of me.

I can picture him clearly, sitting right in front of me, looking at me as if he is a predator, about to devour me like his prey. And deep down, I would let myself feel his sinful touch and kisses. Those rough hands grabbing my thighs and hips with a possessive grip before they wrap around my neck, reminding me he owns me. His lips planting gentle yet passionate kisses all over my body until I am writhing under his arms. That picture is enough to make my thighs press together from the aching and throbbing between my legs.

A sudden knock on my door makes me jolt back to reality as I quickly put back on my veil. When I open the door, it is Julian.

He steps inside and locks the door before standing in front of me. "Did he say something?"

"Who are you talking about?" I question him.

He grabs my jaw tightly and forces me to meet his rage-filled eyes. "You know well whom I'm referring to. He has been in your room for hours." He digs his fingers deeper into my cheeks, that my face aches, but I don't whimper in pain as I try to be strong.

a lovely menace

"What did you two discuss?"

"N-nothing," I struggle to say, "H-he woke up a few moments before y-you k-knocked."

He leans closer with a thunderous look, tightening his grip on my jaw while I try to push away his wrist. "Don't think I'm blind and foolish. I notice the way he looks at you. If you think he will save you or care for you, then you are stupider than I thought," he sneers and pushes me away so hard that I land on the floor on my elbows with a thud.

Before I can recover, I feel a harsh kick against my gut and yelp in pain. Holding onto my stomach, it doesn't stop him from kicking me again and again. I lose count of his attack. My stomach hurts badly as I shiver in pain, and tears blur my vision.

"Ah! Stop!" I cry out in pain, only to get kicked in the face, feeling instant pain radiating through my skull.

"A worthless, useless, weak, and hideous whore. That is what you are, you slut! Remember your place. Nobody will save you here because you have been brought to serve God, not a sinner. Understood?"

I weakly nod my answer, but he kicks me again. "Answer me!"

"Y-yes…I understand," I whisper.

"Good. Now get up and look into Jason. He is in the

underground screaming again," he mutters and then leaves. I slowly get up, tasting the copper taste of blood on my tongue from my cut lips.

For once, I agree with Julian—nobody will save me here. Nobody will care for me…especially when they discover I'm nothing but a monster dressed as a nun, whose dark soul not only mocks this habit I wear and ruins the lives of many innocents in this prison.

And for that, no matter how much I confess, I won't ever be forgiven.

CHAPTER 3

SILAS

The prisoners and I rip the thatch from the ground. It was one of our daily tasks in afternoons while the guards kept watching over us. And after this, we are given lunch before being sent to the confession room.

I work faster so that I could go in first. I have to meet Aella. After being dragged out of her room, I was kept in my cell for the next few days in isolation as punishment for the act I pulled. The only thing I could do was wait; with every passing day, my eagerness to meet Aella increased. However, she didn't come to our floor either, causing me to worry about her.

"All prisoners. Sit on the ground. Your food is on its way," the announcement from the mic on the roof boomed around. We all stopped working and sat down, dusting our hands as the guards brought our food in small wooden boxes.

Crossing my legs, I feel my stomach rumbling from hunger and take the box. Placing it on the ground, I open it and see some soggy rice, barely cooked meat, and a few slices of carrots inside. I'm used to the horrendous food here, so I start to munch down the rice with the spoon, but when I scoop up the meat, I stop halfway to my mouth. A different smell hit my nostrils, making me frown.

What's this smell?

I look around and see everyone eating the meat normally. Then, why does mine smell different? I keep it aside and only have the carrots. Finishing my meal quickly, I close the box and walk to the guard.

"Can I go to the confession room now?" I ask.

"Are you finished with your meal?"

I nod. He looks me up and down before gesturing for me to go. The building is mostly empty as I walk down the hall and take the stairs to the top floor, where the confession room is.

Without knocking, I step inside and exhale in relief when I see Aella's figure on the other side while I take my seat.

"Aella," I mutter her name, noticing that she looks the other way.

My brows furrowed in confusion and without thinking I walk to her side and open the door. As if she didn't expect it from me, her head snaps up and that's when I see her bruised cheeks and cut lips. They look partially healed but still fresh.

Her breathing turns uneven, her eyes widening in surprise. She raises her hand to close the door, but I keep it open with my palm against it. I feel my entire body trembling in anger as I think of the torture she endured without my knowledge.

I kneel in front of her, meeting her at eye level, and cup her face.

"Before you say anything-"

"I need his name," I interrupt her. "Give me his name, and I will bring his heart to your feet."

She is quiet for a while before taking a shaky breath and looking down. "You won't do anything."

I open my mouth to speak, but she raises her hand, gesturing me to stop. "You won't fight or kill anyone because they will put you underground if you do. And trust me; you don't want to be there."

I frown. "Have you been there?" I asked.

Her pupils dilate as if my question trigger her, letting me know her answer. "Aella, just for once, have faith in me. I will protect you with my life."

She smiles weakly, but there is a pain in that smile, which makes my heart ache. "Don't make promises that will put you in danger. I'm not worth it, Silas."

I lean closer to her, gazing into her with intense eyes. Our hot breaths mingle as her gaze shifts from my eyes to my lips. Without thinking, I press my lips to hers for a deep, heated kiss. Her hands grasp my wrists as she joins me and kisses me back with the same passion.

All this time, her morals and the bars kept us apart. But today, neither of us cares. It is forbidden and sinful, yet everything about it feels heavenly.

"Does this feel like you are not worth it?" I said in a low voice against her lips.

She exhales heavily, biting her bottom lip. "You don't even know me, and yet you are willing to sacrifice for me... why?"

"Because when I look at you, I feel a peace that I have never felt. You are the calm to my storm. And to keep that calmness, I will do everything possible to protect it...to protect you, my love."

"What if this peace comes with a price? What if this peace isn't what you hoped for?" she asks.

"I will happily accept it, my love, even if this peace comes with chaos. I will welcome it with open arms. All I ask is for you to trust and open to me—" my thoughts are left unfinished when Aella kisses me harshly. Our tongues dance together as I swallow her moans. My whole body roars with a desire that has been pent up for a long time.

She holds my hand against her jaw, guiding me to hold her there. I slightly lean back and witness her eyes darken when I wrap my hand around her jaw in a possessive grip. I smirk, getting to know this new side of Aella.

Who knew my girl was a little minx underneath her innocence?

Licking her bottom lip, I enjoy the way she whimpers for my touch.

"Sit back and lower your body," I ordered her, and like a good girl, she sits back. Holding onto the hem of her dress, I push it up to her waist and I'm greeted by her flawless, smooth skin. I help her take off her black sandals. Her legs are bare, and her cunt is covered in lacey white underwear, making me groan.

Grabbing her thighs, I part her legs, hearing her pant already. Holding the fabric of her underwear, I push it aside and see her wet cunt.

"Look at that beautiful cunt," I rasp. I trace her slippery pussy lips, earning a moan while she pushes her hips closer to my touch. But I keep tormenting her by gently and lightly circling her clit.

"Silas, please…Oh, god!" she mewls, getting desperate for more.

"You better be prepared not to scream god's name, love, because it will be me taking you to heaven."

I dip my head and lick her cunt. I devour her like a

hungry beast feasting on its prey. Her back arches as she moans with her head thrown back.

I suck on her clit before fucking her cunt with my tongue. Her sweet juices cover my lips and chin, but I savor it all.

"Fucking hell, you taste so good. I could eat you for hours," I groan, continuing fucking her with my tongue. I look up to see her eyes rolling back in pleasure as she fists my hair for leverage.

She looks so divine.

Her legs tremble around my head, with her cries echoing around the room. I increase my speed and push two fingers inside her, intensifying the pleasure for her.

"Ah! Ah! Fuck!" she mewls with her hips gyrating.

"Yeah, just like that. Look at you getting all greedy like a hungry little slut," her cheeks flush with her pussy clenching around my fingers. "Ah, you like that, huh? You like being called my slut?"

She bites her lip, looking all shy and innocent. I sit up slightly and hold her neck with my other hand, pulling her close. "Answer me, my love. Do you like this? Do you like being my little slut who begs for my touch?"

"Yes…please," she whimpers.

"Uh-uh, not like that, my love. I want you to speak up.

Say you want to be fucked hard with my fingers as your juices drip down the floor. Say you want to come and show me how much you love this. Say it," I groaned.

"I...I," she struggles with her words.

"Say it, Aella, and I will reward you with pleasure you never felt before."

"Please, Silas...fuck me hard with your fingers. Make my juices drip down and make me come. Please, please, please," she pleads.

I plant a swift, deep kiss before darkly grinning at her.

"That's my good girl," I praise her. My movements quicken as I fuck her harder and faster with my fingers, and her entire body shivers and trembles.

I kept my hold on her neck, reminding her to keep looking at me. Her cunt clenches and twitches as I can feel her coming very soon.

"Yeah, that's it. Come on, my love. Clench harder and come on my fingers," I thrust my fingers deeper and add two more, increasing my pace, "come for me, Aella. Come," I order her.

She cries at the top of her lungs as she comes. I feel more liquid oozing out of her, and that's when I see her squirting.

Fuck, this is beyond heaven.

I keep fucking her while she squirts, soaking my hand and arm wet with her juices.

"Yes, such a good little slut," I kiss and nibble her cheek, "so fucking good."

I pull out my fingers and quickly work down my pants, taking my raging hard cock that's begging to be inside her. I tap it a few times against her wet cunt, getting it ready for my cock. Her pussy opens for me, and the next second I pushed inside her.

"No, no, no. I can't…please Silas. I can't come again," she whimpers.

"That is not up to you, my love. You are all mine now; if I want you to come a second time, then you will," I grunt.

I hiss under my breath as I thrust in and out. Aella starts to get lost in pleasure again.

"Fuck! Silas! Yes!" she moans loudly, holding onto my arms.

She feels so damn good that it is indescribable. Her walls tightly grip me as I fuck her with all my might. The carnal need to make her mine feels so strong that I can't control the monster within me that wants to possess her. The confessional box thuds and creaks from my vigorous movements, mixing with the sound of our skins slapping. I hike her dress up to her chest, revealing her luscious breasts with rosy nipples. Like the greedy fucker I am, I grope her tits before taking one in my mouth and sucking hard. Her arms wrap around my shoulder as we drown in pure pleasure.

I kiss her passionately before leaning over and grab her hips to fuck her harder as her breasts shake.

"Fuck, I'm going to come," I rasped, feeling her cunt getting warm and tight around my cock. I circle her clit, loving the way she twitched.

"You want my come, my love, huh? You want your cunt dripping with my come?"

"Yes, yes, yes. Please, come inside me, please, I want it."

I smirk at her. "You shall have it, but it better stay inside you. I want you to remember who was fucking you like a possessive beast."

"Oh, fuck! I'm coming," she moans.

"Yes, come, my love. Come."

Her legs tightly wrap around my hips as she reaches her orgasm. With her cunt gripping me so tightly, I can't hold back anymore and come inside her with a grunt.

I swallow deeply as I try to catch my breath. When reality gradually sets in, I slowly pull out of her and watch her place her hand down to cup her pussy not to let my come leak out.

"That's my good girl. Don't let a single drop leak out."

"I won't," she whispers. "I want it in me, and I want more later."

"Oh, you shall have more, my greedy little slut," I mutter and lower my head to kiss her.

shanjida nusrath ali

CHAPTER 4

SILAS

After leaving the confessional, I headed back to my floor and joined others in the line to work on dusting the floors. Luckily the guards didn't clock in for how long I was away as I busied myself in working.

We all worked for hours and when the announcement came through the mic to head to our cell, we started forming a line to go to our beds. We are served the same food as before and the meat smelled awful. Our foods were either served during our field work outside or at the dining room which usually had broken seats or tables.

What the fuck is this smell?

Avoiding the meat, I finish my meal and lie down. The guards come in to take the boxes from us before closing the cell and ordering us to sleep. But it is often hard to sleep with the bright light from the watchtower shining on every cell now and then.

I kept my mind occupied with thoughts of Aella. I never expected my heart would be after a girl again, especially what happened with my first broken marriage. She is a girl who is the definition of innocence to me, as her beauty mesmerizes me every time. If I had known of her existence before, I would have waited for her instead of marrying a woman who framed me and put me through this hell. I still remember the day my late wife brought havoc that changed me forever.

"Susie?" I called out my wife's name in my hoarse voice as I woke up from our bed. My head hurts like hell as I lowered my feet on the floor with my palm pressed against my temple.

What's happening?

The last thing I remembered was having a few drinks with my buddy, Liam, while Susie sat on my lap. We were talking about our college days then everything turned foggy and dark for me the next second.

I looked over my shoulder, expecting my wife to be by my side, I instantly stood up from the bed with a scream of horror. I felt my throat turn dry, and my eyes widened in horror at the sight in front of me.

It was Liam's body, his throat cut, and his blood covered the bedsheet. His lifeless eyes stared at me, and I felt my entire face turning white as snow from utter shock. I started to pant, unable to think, breathe or speak. I looked down and saw my hands covered in blood...in Liam's blood.

Did I...No. No, this can't be.

The door opened suddenly, and Susie walked in. I could

barely see her from the tears blurring my vision and fear clouding me. I expected her to be surprised and horrified, but instead, she looked calm as she headed toward me.

"Good, you are finally awake," she muttered with a smile.

"W-what…" I pointed at Liam's body, "He…Liam…I…" I stuttered. But she gazed at the body before looking back at me while rolling her eyes in annoyance.

"What? Just get it out! He is dead because you killed him. It's as simple as that."

I frowned in confusion. "What are you talking about?"

"We were drinking and talking when you discovered that I am sleeping with your best friend. Then out of rage, you stabbed him to death," she stated. "The blood is on your hands, sweetie."

I shook my head furiously. "No! I could never! And you were…you two…"

My heart shattered as the thought of the woman I loved and cherished hurt me by cheating with my best friend.

"I know you can never kill him, even if you know that. But the police don't. They will never know how I drugged you and later killed Liam. I put you both in the same bed and smeared the blood all over hands, making it look like you did all the crime. For the police you are the killer here,

the culprit. I'm just an innocent, helpless wife who got stuck in a mess. They will never know it was me who killed him"

"W-what? Why would you do that?"

She shrugged. "I didn't need to do all of this, if you didn't make the stupid decision to give away your money alludes as donations to charities when you die. What about me? Those charities already have shit ton of money from other people. I need every single penny from you. But no, you just had to play the kind-hearted man," she sighed, "I can't believe I married a wimp like you."

"But I thought my money didn't matter to you...that you loved me for who I am."

"Whatever. Save you whiny lines-" her words halt when the sirens reach close to our mansion. "Well, that's my cue."

She suddenly tears half of her dress and ruins her hair on purpose, along with her makeup.

"Have a nice time in prison, sweetie. I will take care of your money and everything else, don't worry."

She started running out of the room as the police barged in with their guns raised.

"Help! Help! Please, save me," she started crying in panic, hiding behind one of the officers as she acted like the victim. "He is trying to kill me, too. Please save me."

"Put your hands behind your head. Right now!" the

officer orders me.

"No, no, no. I didn't do anything, it's her. She-"

"I said hands behind your head! Or I will shoot."

At the time, despite being in shock, I had no choice but to give in. She acted like a victim the whole time, recounting the horror of the night in a choked voice to the police officers and lawyers. During the trial at court, she put all the blame on me.

However, I got my revenge eventually. I escaped from the local prison one night, and the first thing I did was visit my darling wife. Her betrayal changed me entirely, and I no longer cared about anyone. She didn't know about how the horrific sight of Liam's dead body traumatized me and haunted me every night when I slept. I had nightmares of my own best friend, even though I knew it I wasn't the culprit here. But I gave her a taste of her medicine. I snuck into her mansion where she peacefully slept. I can recall her screams even to this day which were music to my ears.

Her horrified eyes met mine as she opened her mouth to scream. But I stopped to it by pressing my palm against her mouth and pressing the kitchen knife close to her jugular.

She turned silent and pale, with sweat droplets running down her temple.

I smirked. "Now that I have your attention, I can

continue torturing you."

She gulped. "Silas, please. I-I know what I did was wrong," she tried to touch my wrist to sweeten her words, *"but I'm your wife. You love me, and you won't- Ah!"* Her pleading was left unfinished when I twisted her wrist and slashed the knife across her skin. Blood spurted out as she screamed.

"You ripped out those feelings from my heart, sweetheart. Your husband died the day you betrayed him."

She started sobbing, looking terrified for the first time. "Silas, please. Don't do this. I'm sorry," she weakly smiled, *"Is that what you want? For me to apologize? See? I'm saying sorry."*

I snorted humorlessly. "Your fake apologies won't get rid of the nightmares I have about Liam's dead body. It won't take away the torture I endure day and night in prison by getting bullied and constantly beaten by the officers or other prisoners."

She shook her head nervously. "I'm so sorry you have to go through that, Silas. I wish I could help you-"

"You couldn't help me if you wanted to, sweetheart, because you paid the guards to make sure I am tortured every day. I heard one of them, which makes me hate you more."

Silence greeted me as I saw her face colored with terror like a guilty culprit. But there was no sign of remorse.

"I still have nightmares about Liam's dead body and his blood smeared on my hands. And when I wake up the betrayal you two put me through with your affair breaks me even more. Let me show you how much it hurt me."

She shook her head vigorously. "No, no, no, no, please, Silas. I beg you, please...No!"

Those were the last words I heard from her before I slashed her throat. Even when she was choking to death, I cut her into pieces with a butcher knife from the kitchen. By dawn, I was covered in my dead wife's blood, but the peace I expected never settled. I didn't even escape from the crime scene, knowing my life would never be the same. One of the maids entered her room in the morning and screamed at the sight.

A few minutes later, the police came and took me in. Then I was shifted to Blackwell Prison, stating I was mentally unstable and they transferred me here. But I'm glad I came here; otherwise, I would have never met my sweet and beautiful woman, Aella.

But now that I have promised to protect her, I shall keep my promise. The way she was hurt and how the other prisoners ogle her, I must get her out of here. For that to

a lovely menace

happen, I need to know what keeps her here, where she is no less than a prisoner. What secret has her caged in this place?

As I am in deep thought, lying in my bed, I hear the creaking sound of the lock opening. I sit up and find Aella opening my cell door. I frown and worriedly look behind her in case anyone else is watching.

She quickly works on the lock and opens it, entering the cell before the light from the watch tower can shine on her. She hides beside the corner wall, breathing heavily. She is still dressed in her habit, looking a tad exhausted yet so beautiful.

"What are you doing here?" I whisper as I head towards her. Holding her shoulders, I guide her to my small bed and sit her in front of me, with my back facing the cell so that the watch tower won't discover her. She holds on to my forearms and looks at me with worry written all over her face.

"I just had to come here," she mutters in a low voice.

I hold her face between my palms. "What happened, my love? Tell me."

Did someone hurt her again?

Her face casts down as her nose sniffles. She is crying. I urge her to look me in the eye, letting me be part of her sorrow.

"Aella, please tell me what happened?" I beg her.

She shakes her head. "I…I just…" she starts but closes her eyes as if it is too much for her. Grabbing her hips, I place her in my lap, letting her head rest against my chest as I try my best to protect her from her darkness.

"You have to share your pain with me, my love. Let me have all of you."

"I just…I had a nightmare that I lost you and the thought scares me so much. It felt so real," she whispers.

"Oh, my love, nothing will happen to me when I have you by my side. I won't ever leave you; I promise you."

"I hope you don't, Silas, because I'm scared when you see all of me, you will loathe me."

I look down at her with my brows furrowed. Grasping her chin, I tilt her head as my face paints with seriousness. "You listen to me and listen well. No matter what happens, nothing will change the way I feel about you. No matter what you say or what others say, I will always want you. I agree that no one in this world is perfect. Hell, even I'm not worthy of you. But you are perfect for me, and I will make myself worthy of you, my love. Whatever fears are eating you alive like this, don't let them win. Remember, I'm here for you and will save you."

Her eyes are red, but she stopped crying. "Can I ask you

for something?"

"What does my love want?"

"Kiss me. Make me forget my fears."

Without hesitating, I softly kiss her lips, which soon turn rough and deep.

I caress her cheek with my thumbs while her hands roam over my chest before she slides underneath my shirt to feel my skin. Her touch sets my body ablaze as I groan.

"Fuck, my love. If you keep going, I might fuck you again," I grunted.

"Nothing is stopping you," she whispers against my lips, making me grin.

"Seems like my love didn't have enough."

"It will never be enough with you. Please, Silas."

I look over my shoulder and see the watch tower's light shining on the other side. I quickly help Aella take off her clothes as she sits naked in my arms with the cross-chain dangling around her neck.

Holy fuck.

Only if I could keep her like this all the time.

I hide her in my arms when the light shines into my cell, and after it passes, I stuff the blanket with Aella's clothes, making it look like I'm asleep underneath.

I take her to the corner wall beside the bars, hiding us

away from the watchful eyes. I press her against the wall and kiss her while taking off my shirt. Her hands continue touching my chest and shoulders like she can't control herself. Her lips kiss my neck, making me groan, and before I know it, she turns me around, switching our positions. I was hard as fuck, feeling desire setting my nerves on fire.

I grin at the feisty sight. Aella kisses my neck, skating her way lower, leaving me with her wet kisses and little bites like she is marking me. She eventually kneels, taking my cock in her hand and peaking her tongue to lick the head lightly. I hiss through my teeth with my eyes closed.

She giggles at my cock twitching, carrying a playful expression. I comb my fingers through her hair before grabbing a fistful and tugging her head back.

"You like torturing me, huh?" I whisper. She bites her lip before licking me again.

"Mmm," I groan. "You look so fucking beautiful on your knees. I have seen you pray to God that way, but tonight you will worship me. Won't you, my love?"

She nods, looking up at me with innocent eyes, which only holds this dark desire I never knew of.

"Open your mouth wide. I am fucking your face until your jaw hurts."

Like my good little slut, she opens her mouth with her

tongue out. I grab her hair in a bunch, tilting her head back and pushing my cock inside. I groan instantly but bite my lip to stop it from echoing around.

"Shit," I curse under my breath as I move my hips back and forth, feeling my cock hit the back of her throat. She gags for a moment but starts to breathe through her nose as she adjusts to my size. Spit drools down her chin, coating her breasts and making her look like Aphrodite.

"Fuck, this feels too good," I moan. I keep her head still and fuck her face harder and faster. Her gargling and muffled moans reach my ears, making me increase my speed. I fuck her like my personal slut, and seeing her enjoy it, makes the moment even better.

I pull back, watching her gulp in a lungful of air with a string of spit connecting from her bottom lip to the tip of my wet, hard cock.

"Look at you," I cup her jaw, caressing her bottom lip with my thumb, "getting hungry for my cock. This is forbidden for you, and yet you are begging for it. Shouldn't you repent for your sins?"

I take off the cross-chain from her neck and put it on my cock. Holding my cock, I tap it lightly against her lips as she leans to take more of me, but I keep her head still by her hair.

"Uh, uh. Pray to me, repent to me, my love," I mutter. "And then you shall be rewarded."

"Forgive me, for I have sinned," she whispers, followed by a mewl. I watch her thighs pressing together like she is seeking relief. But that's a poor substitute.

"What sin did you commit, my love?" I ask, breathing heavily and feeling my heart racing.

"I let myself drown in this sinful pleasure. I let my body and soul crave your constant touch…and my heart falls for you. I should have kept my distance from you, but you are irresistible, Silas. For that, it may be sinful for others, but for me, it's pure heaven."

Her confession makes my heart warm and my blood rush faster.

"I feel the same for you, my love. I never thought I'd be falling for another woman, but you made my dead heart beat again. Only you drive me insane, Aella."

I watch her eyes glisten with happiness. "May I be rewarded now? Please."

Oh, when she says it like that, how can I resist?

"Anything for you, my love." With that, I push my cock inside her mouth again and fuck her with fervor. She gags and chortles with tears running down her cheeks. But the euphoria that floats in her eyes is a sight to behold.

Instead of moving my hips, I use her hair as leverage and move her face back and forth, increasing the speed. Throwing my head back, I relish the pleasure coursing through me with my eyes closed.

"Fuck this is beyond words," I mutter in a low voice. I noticed the watch tower's light a few times crossing my cell, but nothing felt suspicious. The fact that I got to fuck and claim my woman among everyone, intensified the sensation even more.

My balls feel full, begging for release. "Fuck, I'm about to come," I groaned. I pull away, stroking myself vigorously and hiss under my breath.

Aella keeps her mouth wide open, letting the spit drip down her chin to her chest, looking eager to have my come. With a deep groan, I release, watching my come spurt on her tongue. She whimpers and shivers, rolling her eyes back like she is coming.

I smirk and slow down my strokes, watching her swallow my come. I kneel in front of her and hold her chin. "Open, show me."

She does as told, and I nod in approval, watching her smile in a haze. "Did my little slut just come?"

Her cheeks flush from my words as she nods slowly. "Just the thought of me fucking and coming in your mouth made you come. You are the dirtiest slut I've ever seen." I kiss a swift, deep kiss. "But you are all mine, my little slut, and I can do whatever I want with you."

She nods with a shy smile. *Still so innocent.*

But I am still rock hard and want to fuck her cunt next. I help her stand up and turn her towards the wall, her back against my chest. I skim my fingers through her drenched folds.

"So fucking wet for me," I kiss her temple and grab her luscious ass before giving it a rough spank. She jolts and bites her lip to stop yelping. I line my cock against her pussy, her chain dangling from my cock. I twist her hair around my knuckles, making her head tilt backward with her back arched.

I push my cock into her wet cunt, thrusting my hips back and forth. Grabbing her jaw with my other hand, I kiss her deeply, swallowing her moans and cries.

I start fucking her rough and hard, my grip tight on her that I might bruise her. But knowing she likes this sweet pain makes me fall for her harder. She is perfect for me in every way possible, and I thank my fate for bringing her into my life.

Our tongues swirled together as I moved my face away for a moment to lick her neck before planting another kiss

a lovely menace

on her rosy lips. I continue fucking her cunt raw, feeling her warm, tight walls clenching around me. She grips me so tightly that I'm going to come again. Lowering my hand from her jaw, I place it on her ass, grabbing it roughly; I hope there would be my fingerprints on it.

I spank her again and again, feeling her grip tighten. She twitches with her body trembling. Her eyes roll back as she drowns in the haze of pleasure. I can feel her mind going blank from desire.

"Is my love about to come? I can feel your pussy gripping me."

She whispers a few incoherent words like she can't speak. I grin and increase my speed. Her mouth slacks open, and her body feels light, as if she is surrendering her whole body to me.

"Fuck! I'm going to come," I whisper against her lips, nibbling her bottom lips.

"P-please…please…need to come…" she whispers her words loosely. Holding her tighter and closer to me, I thrust faster, and after a few deep strokes, I come inside her cunt.

She shivers from head to toe, finding her release. She instantly turns into a puddle, but I keep her in my arms as we both breathe heavily and muffle each other's moans with our kiss.

If this is what heaven feels like, then I never want to leave.

As reality starts to settle back, I gently kiss the side of her face before pulling back. Her cross-chain slips down from my cock with a clang. I help Aella stand straight as my come leaks out of her cunt. I will give her more later.

I carry her in my arms and bring her to my bed. Taking the blanket, I cover both of us, but mostly so the watch tower won't find her. For the next few moments, she lays in my arms, looking flushed and sweaty from fucking, but a soft and gleeful smile crosses her lips, making me savor the moment.

Oh, Aella. I promise to break you out of this prison and give you the life you deserve.

CHAPTER 5

AELLA

I know this will get me in serious trouble. But I have no other way. I need to save Silas before it's too late.

Taking out the bar of soap from my pocket, I press the cell key against it, taking a print of it. Looking over my shoulder, I place the key back on the hook and quickly make my way out of Julian's room. A few guards in the hallway narrow their eyes at me but don't question me as I leave the floor.

When I get closer to my room, I feel relief take over, but Julian's voice makes my steps, and my heart halt for a second.

"Aella," he says my name as I turn around to face him.

I try to control my nerves as he stalks toward me. He looks at me with displeased eyes, as always, as if my sight always infuriates him.

"You need to come to the underground now," he simply states and walks away, knowing well I will follow him. My heart keeps thudding faster against my chest as a sudden nervousness clouds me. No matter how often I visit the underground, it always scares me.

Taking a turn in the hallway, Julian takes a sconce from the wall before opening the wooden portcullis door. We step in, and instant horror engulfs me as I look at Jason's half-cut body bound to a chair. I start breathing heavily, watching his crimson and rotten legs cut up to his knees. His fingers had been chopped off recently, and the crusted blood colored his hands. His face is pale and tired from being tortured for days, but he still has the energy to survive. He slowly opens his eyes, and when he sees us, broken screams come out of his mouth from fear.

"Aaaaah! Leave! Aaaaah!" He looks like a lunatic with wild eyes and screams piercing my ears.

"He has been like this since last night. Take care of it," Julian orders, leaning against the wall beside the door.

Walking towards Jason, I take off my cross-chain necklace with trembling nerves and sweat coating my temple and neck.

"No! No! No! Stay back!" he yells at me, writhing in the chair even though he knows he can't escape. I stand close to him and grab his jaw, forcing his mouth open. Holding the end of the chain, I twist a small cap off it and tilt it to his lips, letting a few drops fall onto his tongue.

Closing off the end of my chain necklace, I cup his face and hold him still. "I'm here, Jason. I'm here," I whisper to him gently.

His pupils dilate, and gradually he stops his protests.

The liquid is doing its job as he stills with an admirable and creepy smile.

"Oh, my angel, you are here," he softly says in a choked voice.

I nodded with a shaky smile, touching his head gently. "I'm here for you, Jason."

"I was in pain," he looked miserable, "I was worried I lost my path to heaven."

I shake my head. "Never. You will be there when you give up everything."

He vigorously moves his head in agreement like my words make him beyond happy. "Yes, yes, yes. I will do it. I will do anything. I want to be back with my sister…I saw her, and I want to be with her."

I look over my shoulder at Julian, who has his arms crossed with a serious look.

"His arms," he simply mutters. Dread thumps against my chest, making my heart pound as I shift my focus back to Julian.

"Give us your arms."

"Take it, take it. Take everything you need. Just let me be with my sister, please."

"Very good," I praised him. "You will be in heaven soon. Have patience."

a lovely menace

Julian steps forward and takes my place. I slowly step back, watching him pull a butcher's knife from his cloak and slash it across Jason's right arm.

He doesn't scream in pain for once. He chuckles like a madman as if the torment makes him happy. It's the drugs. The LSD...the sweet poison, that is bringing him a step closer to destruction.

When blood starts to stream down the chair, I turn around and dash out of the room. I'm no longer needed, but I also didn't want to be there in the first place. I never wanted this, yet I'm forced into it by Julian—my uncle.

The man not only raped my mother but also killed her. And after her, he made me the angel of Ixtal. Just like he did for my mother who was the previous angel of Ixtal. A fucked up and horrendous community formed by my uncle. He believes he can help people get to heaven. It's nothing but a hoax where innocent lives are tarnished and sacrificed.

Just like mine did when I watched my mother die at the age of eight.

I trembled in fear as I watched Uncle Julian cut off my mother's head. My breathing turns shallow and uneven as the urge to throw up becomes stronger. He cut her other limbs, and people surrounded her dead body in a circle. They all joined hands and chanted with their heads held high as they stood naked.

I should have listened to my mother and not followed her. I should have stayed in my room, but curiosity brought me to this massacre.

I pressed my hand against my mouth to stop crying as tears streamed down my cheeks. Uncle Julian smeared my mother's blood on his hands and painted his forehead. He walked around the circle of people and painted them with her blood. He started to chant along with them. His eyes rolled back like he was possessed.

"Accept our offers, oh, Heaven Almighty. Let us be in the gates of heaven. Accept our sacrifice, accept our angel," Uncle Julian shouts, and everyone else repeated. He went to a nearby wall and grabbed a lighted sconce before coming to my mother's dead body and setting her on fire.

I gasped in shock, unable to hold back. I threw up on the floor, feeling sick; I poured it all out while I sobbed. My heart and soul shattered from the loss of my mother and how ill she had been treated...even in death.

The door I was peeking through suddenly opened, and Uncle Julian stood with a vicious look. "We have a little spy here," he snarled, grabbing a fistful of my hair and dragging me inside the room.

"No! Let me go! Please! No!" I screamed, hitting his

arm, but he brought me closer to my mother's burning body. From such a close view, I could see her skin melting and her hair charring.

The sight was beyond horrendous and traumatizing that it would haunt.

"Look at your mother joining heaven. She will take us there, but soon we will need more. I'm glad she had you because you will be our gateway to heaven from here," he mutters close to my ears, making shivers run down my spine in fear.

"No! Uncle, stop this! Please!" I pleaded with him, but he didn't listen. He grabbed my hair and tilted my head back with force.

"Shut up!" he sneered. "You were born for this, and you will fulfill your role. If you think anyone will save you, you are dead wrong. Anyone attempting to help you will face the same consequences as your mother."

My body turned still at his words.

No. God, please. No.

The sight of my murdered mother would never escape my mind. But if I turned out to be the reason for the death of another innocent person, I would drown in guilt and may not find my way back.

"You are the next angel of the Ixtal people. You will take

us to heaven. Accept this life or die like your mother."

I accepted this life...this miserable and horrific life. For years, Julian and I kept manipulating prisoners in Blackwell Prison. Inducing their minds to fall into this fucked up cult with drugs. Their minds are fucked daily with LSD mixed in their food and drinks. Frequently there will be a weak prisoner who would give in easily. Most recently, it was Jason. He confessed to accidentally killing his sister by pushing her from a boat as a joke. I can sense the immense guilt he carried that weakened him.

Based on the final ritual of Ixtal, a weak soul must be sacrificed before an angel is sent to heaven to gain ascension. By using LSD, Julian manipulated the prisoners to think they belonged in heaven and was free from guilt and sins. But that idea never existed. After the sacrifice, the angel is then used for pleasure and later killed to be sent to heaven, while the people around her feed on her body to attain spirituality. The mere thought makes me sick to my stomach.

And Jason isn't the first victim of Ixtal's last ritual. Over the years Julian has killed several weak souls, and he has claimed to see God in his dreams. He said how God praised him for his sacrifices and performing the ritual. He even professed that God encouraged him to continue on this path for his way to heaven is getting closer.

Many have become Julian's victims. But not Silas. I have been trying my best to protect him from the Ixtal. I even sneaked some rotten herbs in his food as the LSD is odorless and tasteless, so that the foul smell would repulse Silas to take a bite. Now I had to help him get out of here.

But now with Jason being dead and used for sacrifice, the ritual is going to happen any day now. I have to get Silas out of Blackwell Prison before the ritual starts.

But will he accept my help when he knows about my truth? Will he hate me? Will he abandon me?

Only time will tell.

shanjida nusrath ali

CHAPTER 6

SILAS

I'm washing myself in the shower, thinking of my plan to escape with Aella, when I hear a sudden commotion—grunts of pain and thudding.

I turn off the shower and wrap a towel around my waist. Opening the door, I see two men fighting on the ground. They aren't simple pushes or light punches. They are smashing each other's heads against the mirror, crushing it to pieces. Blood and bruises covered their faces, but they didn't stop fighting. It's as if they want to kill each other and behave like madmen.

Some other men and I try to pull them apart, but they continue to kill nearly each other.

"Stop it!" I yell at them.

"No! He is going to take away my chance! It will be me! I will be there!" one of the guys with a bald head mutter as blood drips down his mouth.

What is he talking about?

Thankfully the guards come in and separate them, as I assume they will be escorted to the underground. Confusion dawns on me at the absurd situation that just happened. Just then my eyes fall on the sharp shards of glass on the floor. Without thinking, I pick one up and rush to the stall.

I quickly put on my clothes and hide the glass, planning to use it later.

I act normal and get to work around the grounds as usual. Throughout that time, I worked out my plan to escape. After having lunch, I head to the confessional room and find Aella lighting a candle.

Seeing me, she instantly smiles, and we both rush to each other, our lips pressed in a deep kiss.

Fuck I missed her.

Unable to control myself, I grab her hips, digging my fingers deeper into her skin as I pick her up. She wraps her legs around me while I walk us against the closest wall. I smirk at her eagerness to have more of me, relishing her kisses and bites along my neck and jaw before she kisses me fervently.

That's my good girl.

Holding her jaw, I bite her bottom lip, enjoying how her moaning.

"Seems like you missed me, my love," I rasp.

"So much," she whimpers. Tugging my hair, she pulled me closer like she didn't want our kiss to stop.

I place her down as we step back and quickly get rid of our clothes. She hops into my arms again with a giggle, knowing I will catch her.

I take us into the confessional booth as I sit down while she straddles my lap. My hands roam around her curves and arched back, feeling her smooth and soft skin which I will leave marks on. There are a few hickey marks on her breasts from yesterday.

My lips make their way to her neck, kissing and sucking on that sweet spot that makes her moan loudly.

"Ah!" She throws her head back as I move lower and kiss her nipples, biting around her luscious breasts.

"Oh, Silas! Don't stop," she pleads. I land a slap on her ass, earning another moan from her. My cock presses against her wet cunt as she gyrates her hips back and forth. Her juices covered my cock, making it glisten and ready to fuck her.

"Look at that." I wrap my hand around her neck, choking her slightly. *Just how she loves it.*

I urge her to glance between her legs while she whimpers for more.

"Look at the way your hips are moving. The way your cunt is getting wet every time you move against my cock. The thought of me being inside you makes you so eager, huh?"

"Yes. God, yes," she says in a low voice.

"You want more of me, don't you? You want to be

fucked hard and have your pussy oozing with my come. Am I right?"

"I do! Please, Silas," she pleads.

"Then show me, my love. Show me what a beautiful slut you are for my cock. Ride me and take your pleasure."

Her cheeks flush from embarrassment as she looks down. But I tighten the grip around her neck, gesturing her to face me.

"Uh, uh, uh. Don't hide, my love. Let your desire come to light because I want to see it, and it's a part of you that makes me want you more. Now ride my cock," I order her, followed by a slap on her breasts.

Aella leans forward, taking my cock in her hand, rubbing the head back and forth against her pussy lips, making us hiss under our breaths. The next second, she lowers herself onto my cock, shutting her eyes and mewling as she adjusts to my size.

I hold her hips, digging my fingers onto her skin as I hold back the urge to thrust like a ravaging beast. She starts moving slowly at first, but eventually, she goes faster and harder. Need and pleasure clouds my mind as her walls clench around my cock.

The slapping of our skins mixes with our moans. I lean forward and keep sucking on her breasts.

"God, yes! Fuck," she rasps. She moves up and down, tugging my hair and pressing my face close to her chest like she doesn't want to let me go.

"You always like rough and hard with me, don't you?" I slap her ass cheeks again and again, making her yelp. Her eyes are hazy with lust and every inch of her skin turns into a rosy shade.

I grab her head by her neck. "Answer me, my love."

"Yes! Yes! I love it rough and hard with you. Only with you, Silas. I always want to be fucked like this by you," she whimpers.

I land an open-mouth kiss on her lips, our tongues mingling together. Our bodies are sweaty, and our breathing is shallow and harsh.

"Open your mouth," I order, and she does. I spit in her mouth before kissing her again. God, I can never get enough of this…I can never get enough of her.

She doesn't stop, making me grin at my hungry little slut.

Every part of her is fucking beautiful.

Bite marks and fingerprints covers her skin as my chest swells with possessiveness. I know nobody will ever see her like this, and I will make sure no one ever will. She is all mine. Only mine.

I feel her cunt twitching as she gets to the brim of her orgasm. I'm getting close as well. I keep spanking her, knowing well it triggers her orgasm even more. My hands are turning red and achy, but I don't care as long as she comes on my cock.

"Come for me, Aella. Come," I grunt against her lips.

She arches her head back and comes loudly. Her cunt squeezes me tightly. I groan deeply before I spill inside her.

"Fuck, fuck, fuck," I cursed under my breath, pressing my face against her chest as we both came undone in each other's arms. We pant heavily as she sits on my lap.

Gradually, reality sets back, and she sits up. A shy smile crosses her face when we get up to put on our clothes. It's time for me to leave, but I stay close to her and hold her face.

"I love you so much. I'm thankful I have an angel like you in my life."

Tears pool in her eyes instead of being gifted with her smile. I frown in confusion when she suddenly looks pale and nervous.

"Aella, what's wrong? What happened?" I ask her in a serious tone. But she remains silent, making me worry more. I guide her to the booth again and sit her down.

"Aella, please tell me what happened. What did I say?"

Something must have triggered her, and I need to know. I will get rid of all the pain for her.

"I'm no angel, Silas. And I hate that word so much."

I stare in confusion. "What do you mean?"

What is happening?

CHAPTER 7

AELLA

"I need to tell you something, Silas. And I hope that when you know my truth, you won't abandon me." But deep down, I can sense he will.

He grasps my hands, assuring me silently to speak my mind. "Whatever it is, I promise I will keep an open mind."

I close my eyes for a moment, preparing myself mentally before letting out a deep breath as I reveal everything about myself. I tell him every little detail, starting from the very beginning when I first stepped into this hell hole. I keep looking at him nervously the entire time, but he keeps a stoic expression, not letting me know what he is thinking.

I tell him about my mother, my uncle, how he tortured me physically and mentally, how I let many innocent people die because of this fucked up ritual, and how Ixtal ruined my life.

Finally, I remain silent when I finish as anxiety courses through my blood, making me fearful of losing the man I love. But instead of harsh words or disgusted looks, Silas pulls me against his arms and kisses my temple. The gesture surprises me but simultaneously overwhelms me, and I start crying. I circle my arms around his waist, letting out all the sadness I have kept hidden all these years. I finally have someone there for me despite my tough times. My heart feels whole after years of longing.

"Shh, it's okay, my love. It's okay," he whispers against my temple. He touches my head gently, trying to soothe me.

"I'm here for you, my love."

I cry harder and hold him tighter, afraid this is all too good to be true. "How can you even look at me after knowing the things I did? How can you even love me?"

"Because you didn't do them on purpose, my love." He cups my face, urging me to look at him right into his eyes, full of love and care. All for me.

"Your uncle destroyed your life and forced you to do things that you didn't want to do. But despite all of this, you still stayed strong for yourself."

I sniffle. "I tried to escape many times. But somehow, he would find out, or his guards would catch me. He broke my arm once, and for several months I couldn't lift anything."

"Fucking bastard," he curses under his breath. "I'm here now, my love. And I will keep my promise of saving you and getting you out of here. I will protect you and kill any fucker who tries to hurt you."

"I will protect you too, Silas. You mean everything to me. Because of you, I have this new hope I lost long ago."

He smiles softly at me before kissing me. "You give me

the same hope, my love."

I lightly chuckle through my tears as he wipes them away with his thumb.

"We must escape from here as soon as possible. I have worked around the grounds for several months, and I think once we cross the hillside, we can get help. I even managed to get a shard of glass in case we get attacked."

I nodded. "I also got a print of the exit key; in case the doors are locked."

"Good girl." He kisses my forehead. "Let's wait a few days. I will keep track of the guards shifts and rotations. That way we can find the peak time to escape."

"Just be careful. Please. I have already lost so much in my life; I'm not going to lose you either."

Silas shakes his head, gazing at me with determination filled in his eyes. "Nothing will tear us apart, my love. We will escape."

***

Five days later, Silas shares the guards would be gone from their posts for a few hours before dawn. He knows they have a common shift and suggests this would be the best time to escape.

a lovely menace

I go to the rooftop, looking over at the hillsides to get an idea of how long it might take us to get far away from here.

We decided that we are going to escape today. It's nighttime as I finish putting a few necessary items inside my satchel. I left the key to his cell under his bed, so he should be here any minute now.

My door suddenly opens, and who I see instantly makes my body still. It is Julian.

"I didn't expect you to be up so late, Aella," he mutters coldly, closing the door and stepping close to me.

I swallowed, trying to look calm. "I couldn't fall asleep."

"Hmm, is that the reason?" he questions. His hands are behind him like he is hiding something.

I nodded my answer.

His eyes narrow as he gets close to my face. "I don't think so, Aella."

Shit. He knows.

"I'm not a fucking useless and stupid person like you, Aella," he insults me. "When my guards reported that Silas was leaving early from his ground duties for the past few days, I knew something was going on. I surely didn't expect you to be involved in it."

He chuckles darkly with disgust in his eyes. "You really think you can leave with a man who doesn't give a shit about you? He will leave you the second he is out of here. No man will ever want to be with a whore like you, especially when he knows what you have done for all these years."

I don't act anymore this time, but keeping my head high, I respond to him. "He knows everything, uncle. He is aware of every harsh truth about me, yet he chose me," I mutter proudly. "Say whatever you want, but I don't fucking care anymore. You can go and fuck yourself," I curse at him before spitting on his face out of spite.

His face is instantly filled with anger as he grips me by my hair and throws me onto the floor. I grunt in pain and let out a cry when his boots meet my shoulder.

"I have had enough of your bullshit." He straddles me from behind as I thrash out of his hold. His body weight keeps me down while he forcefully grabs my arms and places them behind me.

"Let me go!" I scream. He takes thick ropes out of his back pocket, tying my hands and legs together before standing up. He kicks my head and chest with all his might. Agony instantly burns my whole body.

Julian leans down and holds my jaw tightly. "It's finally time for you to leave, Aella. Tonight, you will do your duties as the angel of Ixtal and be gone from here."

"No," I whispered in horror.

No...He is going to perform the last ritual of Ixtal.

shanjida nusrath ali

CHAPTER 8

AELLA

The moment I have been dreading is here. I tried my best to avoid this disaster, but it found its way back to me one way or another.

Julian drags me by my hair as I struggle against my restraints. I scream and cry in pain as fear makes my heart race. When we reach the stairway, he kicks me in the gut, making me roll down the stairs to the underground. Every inch of me roars in agony, but I try my best to stay strong.

"Because of you, our path to heaven is endangered. You fucking brat!" Julian kicks me across my face before spitting on me.

"Let me go! Silas! Silas!" I scream his name, crying out for help.

But Julian darkly laughs as he forcefully takes me to the omen room, where I hear loud prayers echoing outside...the same prayers I heard when I watched my mother die.

God, please, no! No, no, no.

I wiggle my bound hands, but it's no use. Julian opens the door and hauls me inside, where all the prisoners are sitting in a circle, including the guards. Lit candles surround them and the center. But when I find Silas at the center with his hands and legs bound like mine, my heart is frozen from terror.

"No! No! No! Let him go," I plead to Julian, who only laughs in response.

"You should have thought of this before you decided to go against me." He brings my face closer to his by my hair. I feel he will tear them away from my roots. "One more sacrifice won't hurt. God will be pleased by more."

My eyes widen as the realization hits me. He is going to kill Silas.

SILAS

Seeing Aella restrained with bruises covering her face makes me want to rip apart her uncle's head. I was preparing to leave my cell, but I didn't expect some prisoners to bust in, ambush me, and bring me to the underground. I was beaten and slashed across my chest and back before being restrained with thick ropes.

When I saw the bloody setup down here, I connected the dots, and knew it was the ritual Aella told me about— the final ritual of Ixtal.

Thankfully I have the piece of glass hidden in my back pocket. The moment I came here, I had been trying to cut the ropes discreetly. My wrists are starting to ache, and I can feel my hand bleeding from a few cuts from the sharp edges, but I don't stop.

Julian slaps her face harshly and drags her towards me. My blood boils with rage as my veins pop against my forehead.

She yelps in pain when Julian kicks her again before heading to stand at the end of the room.

"Aella," I whisper her name.

She looks at me with sadness and remorse, making my heart ache for her.

"I'm sorry, Silas. This is all my fault…I-I…I didn't want this to happen to you…I'm sorry," tears stream down her face, "I should have been careful. I'm so sorry, Silas-"

"Hey, hey, hey," I tried to calm her down. Her broken voice stabbed my fucking heart. "None of this is your fault. I will get us out of here, I promise."

She shakes her head. "He will-"

"Tonight, we shall please our God!" Julian announces to everyone, and they stop their prayers in unison, listening intently to Julian. "We shall send our angel to God and get a step closer to heaven."

Fuck.

I look at Aella, whose face looks white as snow. She closes her eyes tightly as if she is accepting this miserable ending. But before I can say something, I notice that her hands are close to the candles. I frown and slightly lean forward to see she is trying to burn the ropes.

That's my girl.

Pride swells in my chest, seeing her fight for her freedom even when there is no way out of here.

I work faster on my restraints as well. Julian steps towards Aella. He grabs her jaw, forcing her mouth open.

"No! Fucking stay away from her!" I threaten him. "I will cut you into pieces and feed you to the vultures," I sneer at him with a thunderous expression. Rage courses through my veins as he laughs like the sadistic lunatic he is.

"I will make sure you die slowly," he snickers at me, before shifting his focus back on Aella. He tugs off her cross-chain necklace, and opening the end, he forces the vial of drugs into to her mouth. She moves her face away, but he grabs her jaw tighter.

He steps back as Aella coughs and tries to spit out the drug.

I increase my speed, and thankfully, I feel the ropes loosening. Julian stands close to Aella starts to rip off her clothes, tearing down the rest of her habit.

"Hey! You motherfucker! I am going to kill you!" I yell at him like a vicious beast.

Aella cries and writhes, but that doesn't stop her uncle

from leaving her naked body for others. The men around start to rise, take off their clothes and go for Aella…my love.

Tears of agony and sudden anxiety blur my vision.

No, I beg you God. Help us…help her. Don't taint her like this.

I never pleaded to God but for her I did, hoping for a miracle to save us.

Luckily, God listened to my prayers, freeing my hands from the ropes. I instantly get up and push away the closest man. By then, Aella's ropes also come loose from the flame, and I help her.

"No! Don't let them escape! Hold that bastard down," Julian orders the men. I am suddenly pressed to the ground with harsh punches to my face.

"You won't take away our chance," one of them says before landing a punch across my face while another person harshly stomps on my elbow.

"Fuck!" I grunted in sheer pain. But when I look up, I see Julian and some other men holding Aella down, trying to take off the rest of her clothes.

"No!" I scream, and I snap. Adrenaline rushes through me as I push back the men holding me down. They stagger back but try to rise again. I hit some of them with the back of my elbow, swallowing the excruciating pain radiating

a lovely menace

through my arm. I headbutt a man and punch another.

I'm like a wild beast, fighting with all my power and will. I don't care if everyone dies as long as Aella is safe. I rush to her and kick Julian's chest, making him fall backward with a grunt.

"Fucking stay away from her!" I growled at the men while punching and pushing them away from my love before they break her. Aella quickly tries to cover herself with her tattered clothes and moves away from them.

"Run!" I order her frantically. But I'm pulled back by the men as they mount me, kicking and hitting me without pause. I try my best to hold them off, but the pain takes over my body, turning me weak. My head aches so badly that my vision turns unclear.

I hear loud screams, but the screaming quickly amplifies. *What is going on?*

The surrounding prisoners scatter, screaming and afraid. I shake my head as I get up with a grunt. I find Aella carrying a sconce and setting some men on fire—they scream about being burned alive. As the burning men run around, they bump into others, lighting them on fire.

From the corner, I see Julian looking at this chaos with wild eyes as anger takes over his face, and he strides to attack Aella. I go after him and pin him down from behind.

"Not so fast, fucker," I mutter through my clenched teeth. Holding him by his hair, I keep smashing his head against the concrete ground. I don't stop when I notice the floor is covered in his blood or even when his face is unrecognizable. Looking over my shoulder, I grab one of the flaming candles and pull Julian's head back.

"This is for hurting my girl." I plunge the flame into his eyes, and he screams at the top of his lungs. His body struggles with the pain, but I press the candle deeper. I quickly grab another candle shoving it in his other eye, intensifying his pain.

"Ah! Ah! Ah!" one of the burning prisoner's screams makes me glance up as he staggers towards us. I get up quickly as the burning man falls on Julian, burning the fucker along with him.

"We have to leave. Now!" Aella comes to my side, taking my hand. Within minutes it is nothing but burning bodies around us as we rush out of the room. Keeping the sconce with her, she guides us from the underground and towards the upper floors.

"Where is the exit?" I asked her breathlessly as we ran.

"I remember it," she answers, taking us across a hall as we walk past the watchtower, which is no longer rotating. The entire place is empty, with all the guards and prisoners burning to death.

Aella finds the exit door; without wasting time, we open it and run as fast as possible. We hold each other's hands tightly and escape from this fucked up hell hole. Our breathing turns heavy and shallow as we ignore the pain in our bodies. All that matters is getting as far as possible from this place. Neither of us knew the direction as mountains and hills surrounded us. But when we reached a distance where we could not see Blackwell Prison anymore, we stopped.

We both heaved heavily. I coughed, feeling my lungs burning for air. I glance at Aella and quickly give her my shirt.

"Take this," I tell her. She takes it and covers herself before gazing at me. Her face is covered with cuts and bruises, and her eyes are swelling. But despite all the torment, a small smile crossed her lips…a soft and calming look passes her face as if, for the first time, she feels all the troubles lifting from her shoulders.

"It's all over?" she asks.

I nod, offering her a smile before pulling her into my arms. "It's over."

She sighs and hugs me tighter and resting her head against my chest, finding comfort in my arms.

"What do we do now?" she questions, tilting her head back to look at me.

"We start a new journey and see where life leads us. As long as you are part of this journey, I can carry the hope of a long and beautiful life."

"I will be a part of it…I want to be a part of it because I need you, Silas. You are my everything. I was scared I would lose you, but fate gave us a new chance. And no matter what, I will never let you go," she murmurs.

"I won't either, my love. You will always be my girl and I will follow you anywhere you lead me." I kiss her forehead.

"We should keep walking," I tell her. This time we walk at a slower pace, and walk for hours until we see a road.

We look at each other with hopeful smiles, holding our hands tightly and gesturing silently to our new beginning.

Aella and I walk along the road when we hear a car coming in our direction. I stand in the middle and wave my hand, gesturing for the car to stop. The light blue Chevrolet Cavalier halts and we both rush towards it. There is a man and woman inside, possibly married from the rings on their fingers.

The man carries a sharp and serious look, assessing me like I'm a threat to them. The woman however holds a confusing and worrisome expression, especially glancing at the bruises and scars we have on our faces.

"Can we help you?" the man asks in a cold voice.

I bring Aella closer to me, putting my arm around her shoulder. "Yes. I was thinking if you can take us to the urban side of Vailburg? We are lost," I answer.

"You two don't seem lost to me." He narrows his eyes at us.

"Eryx," the woman calls the man's name over her shoulder in a reprimanding tone.

"Agatha, we can't trust strangers on the road," he states directly, not caring that we could hear him.

"Please. We just need to get to the town side of Vailburg and then we will be on our way from there," Aella mutters, looking at Agatha, pleading to her indirectly for help.

Agatha nods as if she can understand our situation and looks at Eryx. "We should help them. It's just a drive towards the town side."

Eryx looks back and forth from his wife to us as if he is contemplating his decision. But he eventually agrees with a sigh. "You can sit at the back."

"Thank you so much," Aella says with a soft smile.

Opening the door, we get in the back seat as I pull Aella against my chest. Eryx starts the engine and drives away. The windows are rolled down, letting the gust of wind caress our faces with our hair swaying along with it. My eyes glances over the hills we pass by when the distant sight of Blackwell Prison catches my attention for a fleeting moment before it's gone…gone forever.

"Here, you can use this," Agatha passes Aella a shawl. She takes it with a thankful smile and wraps it over her torn clothes. I kiss her temple, wrapping my arms around her.

Our dark past is behind us. No more imprisonment and no more hiding. I don't know what we will do when we reach the town side. I don't know what our lives will be like. But I did know it will be a beautiful and peaceful one with Aella by my side.

Our journey may have started in darkness and menace but it was worth it, as our fates brought us together making it all…*a lovely menace.*

THE END

Did I mention Eryx and Agatha have their own story set in a mental asylum? What happens when Agatha gets kidnapped to an abandoned island and gets involved in a forbidden, steamy and intense relationship with one of the priests there?

Read THE DEVIL TAINTED US (A GOTHIC, AGE GAP AND FORBIDDEN ROMANCE) to dive into the dark, horrifying, forbidden and suspenseful world of the Magdalene.

THE DEVIL TAINTED US Blurb

Mery Heights has been known for its myth of being cursed by God because of the uncountable sins the island carried. But sin is like a shadow inked with the darkness in Magdalene asylum.

When an innocent soul like Agatha is brought to this living hell, she is pushed into the fire of torture, guilt and shame. But she is determined to find her door to freedom and the key was one of the priests of the Magdalene who is no less than a sinner.

Eryx.

The longer Agatha is held captive the more she is drowning into the darkness of the island. But even in the depths she feels an undeniable connection and attraction to Eryx, who can't resist the beautiful and alluring angel.

But soon secrets are revealed, past dig their way out of the graves, endangering their lives. A journey of betrayal, guilt, love and passion with an angel and a sinner fighting for what they yearn before they are tainted by the devil.

Tropes
-Dark, Gothic Romance

-Age Gap

-Forbidden Romance

MORE FROM THE AUTHOR

Shanjida Nusrath Ali is an English major student by day and an aspiring independent author by night. Known for her mafia romance book, Cross My Heart, she loves to write about characters going through a dark and heartbreaking path to love with consequences at every turn and coming out stronger in time. She likes to dip her toes in various tropes to give unique stories to her readers with every new book. Whether its dark romance between a bad boy and a blind ballerina, or a patient falling for a priest in an abandoned mental asylum, Shanjida's stories has intense and jaw-dropping plots that keeps the readers hooked in every page.

Books

Cross My Heart

Kingdom of Sinners (Bitter Love Duet #1)

Kingdom of Redemption (Bitter Love Duet #2)

The Devil Tainted Us (A Gothic, Age Gap and Forbidden Romance)

Deviant Vows (The Quarter Chronicles #1)

Socials

a lovely menace

Made in United States
Troutdale, OR
07/29/2024